PUFFIN BOOKS

GHOSTS AT LARGE

The open road is a hazardous place for the lonely traveller – the Devil is on the loose and the Grim Reaper stalks the land. And from Icelandic farmhouse to Underworld, strange happenings are afoot. Infernal monsters haunt the house over the Hell-crack, while the Headless Boggart gives drunken Jack the fright of his life and an evil old witch disrupts a wedding feast. But fearless and cunning mortals do get their chance to outwit spooks, ghouls and the Devil in his many guises . . .

Here are a dozen beautifully retold traditional stories, ranging from the humorous to the eerie, all fascinating fuel for the imagination.

SUSAN PRICE

Ghosts at Large

Illustrated by Alison Price

PUFFIN BOOKS
in association with Faber and Faber

Puffin Books, Penguin Books Ltd, Harmondsworth, Middlesex, England
Viking Penguin Inc., 40 West 23rd Street, New York, New York 10010, U.S.A.
Penguin Books Australia Ltd, Ringwood, Victoria, Australia
Penguin Books Canada Ltd, 2801 John Street, Markham, Ontario, Canada L3R 1B4
Penguin Books (N.Z.) Ltd, 182–190 Wairau Road, Auckland 10, New Zealand

First published by Faber and Faber Limited 1984
Published in Puffin Books 1986
Reprinted 1986, 1987

Made and printed in Great Britain by
Richard Clay Ltd, Bungay, Suffolk
Typeset in Sabon

Contents

Fearless Mary

There was once a girl named Mary, and everyone used to call her "Fearless Mary" because there wasn't anything that could scare her, and never had been, from the time she'd been a toddler.

She worked for a farmer. She would do any work. The farmer liked her and became fond, even proud, of her. One dark and windy winter's night, he and a friend of his were sitting by the fire in the kitchen, talking and drinking, and they ran out of beer. "Mary," said the farmer, "are you doing anything in particular, love?"

"No," said Mary.

"Well, then, will you nip down to the Old Bush

and fetch us another jug of beer? I'll give you a shilling for your trouble."

Mary got up and was fetching her shawl when the farmer's friend said, "You can't ask a young wench to go all the way down there on her own at this time of night! Her'll be frightened."

The farmer laughed and said, "Will you be frightened, Mary?"

"No," she said. "Give me the jug." And she took the jug and went out into the dark and wind.

While she was away, the farmer began to boast about her. "She cares for nothing," he said. "Bolder than tigers."

Mary was away for a long, long time. "She's got into the pub, where it's light and there's people," said the farmer's friend, "and she's afraid to come out again. *I* don't like being out in the dark. Stands to sense a little wench is going to be scared."

"Ar," said the farmer. "You wait and see how hard she's run through being scared."

When Mary did come in, there wasn't a drop of beer spilt, or a hair of her head out of place, and her breathing was easy and slow, as if she'd just dawdled along.

"Farmer's been telling me you're not scared of anything, living or dead, Mary," said the guest. "Is that right?"

"Oh, I suppose so," Mary said, and held out her hand for the shilling the farmer had promised her. He leaned over in his chair to get it from his pocket, and gave it to her. Then she went to bed.

The farmer and his friend sat on, drinking the beer and talking. The guest would not believe that Mary was fearless, and kept suggesting things that might frighten her. Mice, he said, spiders, and fierce dogs. The farmer said that none of them would bother her at all, and he bet his friend five pounds that he could not think of a task that Mary would be frightened to carry out.

When the beer was finished, the friend went home. That night, and for several nights after, he tried to think of a frightening task, an unnerving task, something that the most courageous man he knew would be timid about performing; and at last he thought he had invented one. To make sure that it would be as frightening as possible, he went to see the sexton of the parish church, made a bargain with him, and borrowed from him the key of the charnel-house. The charnel-house is the place in a church where dead bodies were thrown.

When he went to drink with the farmer again, he said, "I'll win the five pound. I've thought of something your 'fearless' Mary won't do. This is the key to the charnel-house. I bet Mary won't go to the church by herself, at midnight, open up the charnel-house, and fetch us back a skull-bone."

"And I bet she will," said the farmer, and he called Mary and told her what they wanted her to do. "Why not?" she said, and put the key in her pocket, and went about her work until it was midnight. Then she put on her shawl and bonnet, lit a small lantern, and said, "I'm just off to fetch that skull-bone you wanted.''

She walked down the long, sunken lane to the church. It was cold, and dark at the bottom of the lane, and a breeze shook all the leaves of the trees and rattled all the grassheads together. The high banks on either side of the lane trapped the sound of her feet on the hard dirt and whispered them back to her, as if someone was following. Her lantern, being covered to stop the candle being blown out, gave hardly any light at all: just enough to flicker on a tree-bole or gate-post and appear as a sudden movement.

But Mary knew what all the sounds and flickers of light were, and she went right on, at an even pace, without stopping, until she reached the church. She pushed open the heavy old door and went inside, and then she had to stop, for the darkness was complete, and the cold intense and sudden, like a drenching. She opened the door of her lantern, and the yellow light of her candle glimmered over the surface of the darkness. Mary stood still, waiting for her eyes to grow used to the dark. The silence was so deep, and yet so full of tiny, scarcely heard noises, that it was like a long breath.

Mary moved on, with one hand stretched out before her, feeling her way to the door of the charnel-house. Every step she took brought cold echoes from the church roof before the silence breathed again. She found the door and took the key from her pocket, felt for the key-hole, put the key in and turned it. She pushed open the door and went down the steps into that cold, dark, damp place that stank of graves and age.

There were many bones lying on the floor, whole skeletons and broken ones: ribs, thigh-bones, spines and skulls. Mary shone her lantern over them and moved some with her foot, until she saw a skull that had been broken away from its spine. She bent to pick it up. As she did so, a voice cried out, a deep, dull voice, like the voice of someone speaking into his cupped hands. It said, "Let that bone be; that's my mother's bone."

Mary stopped. "Oh," she said. "All right." She moved on into the charnel-house, going further from the door, shining her lantern until she saw another skull. She picked it up.

"Let that bone be; that's my father's bone," the deep voice cried out again.

"Well, all right, if it's your father's bone," Mary said, and she dropped the skull because she could see another one close by, easy to pick up.

"Let that bone be," the voice began. "That's my – "

Mary lost her temper. "Father's, mother's, sister's, brother's," she said. "I must have a skull-bone, and this shall be it!" Carrying the skull, she stamped back through the bones to the charnel-house steps, slammed the door behind her, locked it, and put the key in her pocket.

A tremendous racket broke out behind her. Something was banging on the inside of the charnel-house door, and something inside was howling and wailing in a most disturbing and dismal way. "Screech away, old ghost," Mary said. "Bang all you like. I'm taking this skull to farmer – but I might bring it back tomorrow night, if it upsets you so much."

And then she went home, strolling along the dark, sunken lane with the skull under her arm. When she reached the farmhouse, she put the skull on the table beside the guest's beer-mug. "There's your skull-bone," she said. "Now let's see your five pounds."

The farmer's friend started away from the skull. "But didn't you *hear* anything, Mary, while you were in the charnel?" he asked.

"Oh ar. There was this old ghost maundering on about his Daddy's bones and his Mammy's bones, but I told him straight that I wanted a bone and I was taking one."

"Ar, but – didn't the ghost say anything else, Mary?"

"No ... But after I'd locked the charnel-door again, it didn't half holler and shriek. The way it banged on the door, you'd have thought it was a living man."

The farmer's friend stood and counted five pounds on the table. "Give me the charnel-key back, Mary, love," he said. "I'd better hurry and let sexton out." He was going when Mary thrust the skull into his arms, saying,

"Well, since you've got the key, you can just put the skull back for me."

The guest was so alarmed at being asked to hold

the skull that he almost dropped it on the stone floor, and Mary had to catch it; but at last he went off, carefully carrying the skull in the crook of his arm, so that only his clothes touched it.

Mary said to the farmer, "I fetched the skull, so that five pounds is mine by rights." She pocketed it, and he didn't say her no.

This story of Mary and the ghost in the charnel-house soon spread about the country, and was heard by another farmer, who lived some miles away. Now, the mother of this farmer had recently died, but she hadn't left his house. Her ghost kept returning. Sometimes it was fully visible, sometimes it was visible only above the waist. It came most often at meal-times, and would sit at the table and move a knife and fork just as if it was eating. This frightened everyone in the house, and within a couple of weeks all who could leave had left, and the farmer was alone with all the work of both farm and house to do himself. He came to see Fearless Mary, told her all about his mother's ghost, and asked her if she would be afraid of it.

"Well, no," she said. "Why should I be? I pay no regard to ghosts."

"Will you come and work for me, then?" he asked. "Cook, clean, keep house?"

"I've got a good place here," said Mary.

"I'll pay you more," said the farmer.

"Three times as much?" Mary asked. "Three times as much, or you can keep your own house."

The farmer had to agree, and Mary went to work

for him. The ghost appeared on her very first day, invisible from the waist down, and hovered above a chair at the table, just as if it was sitting on it. "Good day, Missis," Mary said, and took no further notice of it, but went on with her work. She set the table, and laid a place in front of the ghost, and when she served up dinner for herself and the farmer, she put a little food on the ghost's plate; and she offered it bread and butter, salt and sauce.

"Why do you do that, Mary?" asked the farmer. "She's a ghost."

"It's only polite," Mary said, and she treated the ghost in the same way whenever it appeared at meal-times. If it came while she was working round the house or yard, she just smiled, said, "Good day, Missis," and got on.

The farmer had gone to market one day when the ghost suddenly appeared to Mary as she was cleaning the cooking-range and, for the first time, spoke to her. "Are you afraid of me, Mary?" it said.

"No," Mary said. "You're dead, and I'm alive."

"Then come down into the cellar with me and I'll show you something," said the ghost.

Mary followed the ghost down into the cellar. It floated across to the wall and pointed to some floorboards. "Take those up," it said. Mary did so and in a hole underneath were two bags, one large and one small. "The big bag's for my son," said the ghost, "and the little one's for you, because you're a hard-working, fearless girl, Mary, and deserve it." Then the ghost vanished.

Mary put the floorboards back, left the cellar and went on with her work until the farmer came back. She told him about the ghost's appearance, took him down into the cellar, and showed him the bags under the floor. The farmer lifted out the smaller one, and opened it. It was full of gold.

"Your mother's ghost said that the little one was for you, and the big one for me," Mary told him.

The farmer frowned. "Are you sure that's right, Mary? Didn't she say the big one was for me?"

"No, not at all, she said the *little* bag was for you."

"Well, if that's what she *said* ..."

"It was, because if it hadn't been for me being so fearless, you wouldn't have any gold at all, and you've enough to be going on with in the little bag. By the way, you'd better look round for another maid."

This was good advice, because the next day Mary took all her gold to town and banked it, and set herself up in a house of her own. For the rest of her long and happy life she lived there, doing just as she liked, in the greatest comfort.

Death and the Soldier

There was once a Russian soldier who, for ten years, had fought for his Tsar on battlefields at every border of Russia, and in other countries too; but as soon as the wars were over, and soldiers weren't wanted any more, he was turned off without a penny in wages. He started walking, with a knapsack on his back as empty as his pockets. He was going home. Along the way he begged and stole, when he could; and he sold his boots to get money for food, and wrapped his feet in rags instead. He slept in hedgerows and in barns, and soon his long greatcoat was torn and rotting, and he looked like any other beggar. And it was still a long way home.

He came to a town where there was a grand house with high roofs and many windows and chimneys. He was wondering who was lucky enough to live there when he realized that it was empty. No smoke came from the chimneys; no curtains hung at any of the windows, and no one was to be seen in the yard. Funny, thought the soldier, when so many people are homeless, to have a big house like that standing empty.

He stopped at the Inn and spent some coppers he had worked for on vodka; and he grumbled to the landlord about the empty house.

"It's empty for a good reason, that place," said the landlord.

The soldier asked for the story.

"We all told him not to build there," said the landlord. "But would he listen? There's a crack in the ground under that house, a crack that goes right down to Hell. Every night the house is full of demons and bugaboos."

"You don't say," said the soldier.

"Nobody can stay in it," the landlord went on. "The servants are sent in before the Master, to get the place ready for him – and the next day they're found scattered in every room with all their bones broken."

"All their bones broken, eh?" said the soldier, and looked down at the sodden rags on his feet. "Isn't it always the working man that suffers?"

"So you see, nobody's ever lived in it," said the landlord. "People have tried from time to time – priests have tried – but it's always the same."

The soldier stood. "Who owns this house, Captain, and where does he live?"

"What do you want – you're not going to try, are you?"

"Well, listen," said the soldier. "I fight for the Tsar for ten years and what's my reward? Nothing. So I'm going home to my parents in the Ukraine, and what is there for me there? Nothing. So, reckoning my chances in this world, I may as well take my chances with the next." And when the landlord had told him where he could find the owner of the house over the Hell-crack, he touched his cap and marched off.

He found the owner's lodgings, and was taken in to see him; and when the owner asked what he wanted, the soldier said straight away that he wanted to try to rid the big house of its devils, and how much was the reward if he succeeded?

"Do you know how many people have been killed – or worse – trying to do that?" asked the rich man. "What makes you think you can turn the trick?"

"I'm not sure I can," said the soldier. "But even if you offer no more than ten roubles for the job, it's a better chance than I'll find elsewhere in the world – and if they break my bones, well, I have to die some time. At least I'll have a roof over my head for a while – until Hell turns out! So how about it, sir? Ten roubles?"

"I'd give ten thousand roubles to anyone who could make the place safe," said the owner.

"How much?"

"Ten thousand roubles!"

The soldier clapped his hands together. "Now that's a sum worth dying to earn!" he said, and with his empty knapsack on his back, and the rags round his feet coming undone and squelching, he went back along the road to the great, empty house, and settled down for the night in one of the grandest of its rooms, a ballroom with gilded doors, painted walls, and shining, glittering chandeliers let down on their chains so close to the marble floor that the soldier had to walk between them.

He took off his knapsack, laid it on the floor close by, and sat down in a corner to wait. The room grew darker and darker, and colder and colder. The whole house was already so quiet that he had been glad to find somewhere to sit down, so that he no longer had to listen to his own footsteps echoing through the passageways.

He knew when midnight came because, deep down in the ground beneath the house, there began a quivering and a rumbling and, in the midst of it, a shrieking and a laughing; and it all grew louder and louder until, in through the walls and doors, up through the floors, there burst bugaboos, gringes, clabbernappers, bonelesses, ghouls, brugs and shocks. They seized each other by whatever was nearest – hand, ear, horn, nose, tail or blob – and they danced like the fiends they were. But when they caught sight of the soldier sitting quietly in the corner, they were all silent in an instant, every one of them, and trembling with eagerness. One among them cried out, "Meat; fresh warm meat for the party!"

"And bones to crack and suck!" called another.

The rest joined in with a hullaballoo of yells, screams, squeaks and yelps; and they all moved together towards the soldier.

The soldier got slowly to his feet. He drew his ragged greatcoat about him, and adjusted his cap. He straightened his shoulders, advanced one foot and, as the mob came very near, he shouted, "Boo!"

They all jumped and backed off. The soldier smiled and, even louder than before, he shouted, "Boo!" again. The devils scratched, clattered and leaped over, under and through one another until they were all crammed in the far corner of the room. They peered timidly at the soldier. No one had ever said "Boo!" to them before.

The soldier was pleased with himself, and he tipped his cap again. He slung his knapsack from his shoulder by one strap, and he swaggered between the chandeliers to the crowd of monsters. "People told me you'd be frightening," he said, "but they must have been people who'd never been to war. Now I've been a soldier for ten years, and I've seen worse sights than you on every battlefield I've fought on."

A ghoul looked out of the crowd and said, "Then how can we scare you, like we're supposed to do?"

"I don't know if you can, after the things I've

seen," said the soldier. "You Bonelesses – I can tell you, you'd be more frightening if you *had* bones. And Shocks? I've had every kind of shock there is ... But there was *one* thing I was told about you that impressed me..." The devils all crowded closer. "I was told that you could all, every last one of you, make yourselves as big as mountains – "

Every devil in the room, on all sides, began to swell and stretch and grow, and the soldier had to shout out quickly, as loudly as he could, "But that wasn't what impressed me *most!*" All the devils stopped growing for the moment and listened. "What impressed me *most* was that they said you could all make yourselves as small as flies, so small that the whole horde of you could fit – well, could fit into this knapsack of mine, for example." He took it from his shoulder and opened it. "Now I don't believe that, and if I were to see it with my own eyes – " Before he could finish speaking, with excited squeals and frightening laughter, all the devils rushed towards the open mouth of the knapsack, shrinking as they went. The soldier laid the knapsack on the floor, and stood aside and watched. It was a wonderful sight. The knapsack heaved and moved as it filled with demons, and there were still hundreds of them to fit into it, but in seconds they grew small as flies, and smaller; smaller than midges, smaller than dust specks. And when they were all inside, the soldier jumped on the knapsack and fastened it up tight. He worked quickly, for he had been astonished by the devils' power, and he did not want them to get out. He took off his greatcoat and wrapped the knapsack tightly in it; and then he used the whole bundle as a pillow while he dozed away the rest of the night. He slept with the buzzing of Hell in his ears.

The next morning he carried the bundle into the town. People came running from all the houses to see him pass, for the landlord had spread the news that yet another fool had gone to get his bones broken in the house over the Hell-crack. Everyone was surprised to see the soldier still alive, and many followed him to see what he was going to do.

The soldier went to the blacksmith's forge, and he put his bundle on the anvil. "Do this small thing for me," he said to the blacksmith. "Give my old knapsack here a good hammering. I shall be coming into a fortune soon, and I'll pay you well for the favour."

So the blacksmith took his big hammer, and his son took up another, and they both began to beat the soldier's knapsack – but they stopped short in horror at the screaming, screeching din which came from it at their first blows. "Beat on," said the soldier. "I filled it at the place I stayed last night."

Then the blacksmiths guessed what was in the sack, and they began to hammer it furiously; and other people crowded into the forge and took hammers and spikes and belaboured the knapsack too; while the soldier stood in the forge door and watched.

The screams were so loud they were heard in Hell,

and the soldier soon felt a tap on his shoulder. He turned to find Lucifer himself standing just behind him. "What will you take in return for letting my people go, soldier?" Lucifer asked.

The soldier spoke up immediately. "I'd like a knapsack," he said, "just like my old one, but with these qualities: that whatever I ask it to hold, it will hold; that whatever I command to get inside it, must get inside it; and that whatever is inside it can't get out without my permission."

"That is easily done," said Lucifer. "You might have asked for much more. But may I make this condition? That it will be impossible for you to throw away this wonderful knapsack?"

"Certainly you may," said the soldier. "I won't ever want to throw it away."

Lucifer nodded and sank through the ground. A second later, he rose up again, and handed the soldier a knapsack. Then he snatched the knapsack from the anvil and sank through the forge-floor, returning to Hell with his people.

As the crowd pressed back from the anvil in astonishment, panting and gasping from their exertions, the soldier clapped his hands and said, "I'm just off to fetch my reward." He fastened on his new knapsack. "And then I'll buy you all a meal and a drink before I go on my way." So all the people left the forge and followed him to the lodgings of the rich man who owned the house over the Hell-crack. They waited outside.

When the soldier was shown in, the rich man said,

"Ah! So you didn't spend the night in my house after all?"

"Yes, I did," answered the soldier. "I served those devils as they deserve and now they're so sore, I don't suppose they'll ever come back to that particular spot on earth. I've come for that ten thousand roubles you promised me."

"Oh, you don't think I believe your tale, do you?" asked the rich man.

"I don't see why not, since I'm telling the truth," said the soldier. "I'd be grateful if you'd give me my money, so that I can be on my way."

"You won't get one rouble out of me, not for all your fairy-tales," said the rich man.

"I could serve you as I served the devils," said the soldier thoughtfully. "But I won't. Will you at least admit that you promised me the money?"

"As a joke, yes. But only because I knew you could never earn it."

"That's all I want to hear you say," said the soldier, and he left the rich man's lodgings. Thank God he's gone, thought the rich man. The soldier stood outside on the stairs and he said aloud, "Knapsack! Hold ten thousand roubles of this man's money." The knapsack immediately became very heavy on his back. He took some of the money from it and put it in his pockets, and he went down the stairs and bought food and drink for all the people of that town. When the party was over he slept in the best room of the Inn, and the next morning he bought himself new, fine clothes, and new boots; and he travelled on to his home by coach.

When he reached his home, he bought himself a farm, and he married. Some years passed, and he and his wife had three children, and were as happy together as any couple ever are. He was glad that he had risked his life that night in the house above the Hell-crack, because otherwise he would have had none of the good things that brought him contentment now. But then he fell ill.

For ten days he lay in bed, and his family were sure he would die, he was in such a fever. But after ten days the soldier began to come to himself, and to feel much better. It was then that he looked up and saw a stranger sitting by his bedside. This stranger was so thin that his bones couldn't have been seen more clearly had he been a skeleton. A coarse, filthy old cloak that stank of earth and damp hung round him and, in his bone-and-tendon hand he held a scythe. It was Death.

"Out of that bed," Death said. "Now you must come with me."

"Yes, but not yet," said the soldier. "I can't be meant to go yet – I'm still young – I have things to do – my children aren't half-grown."

"Hurry," Death said. "I'm hungry."

"Look, give me a few more years," said the soldier. "I needn't go straight away, surely?" Death shook his head. "A few months then? A few weeks? Days? Surely just another hour?" Death shook his head at each suggestion. "Just a few minutes then," the soldier begged. "Let me call my wife and children. They'll come and look in at the door – let me – "

"No more time!" Death shouted. And he seized the soldier by the wrist and dragged him from the bed. As he fell, the soldier saw the knapsack hanging on the bedpost. He reached out and grabbed it, and yelled, "Death! Get into the knapsack!"

Then Death fell under the Devil's power, and he couldn't help himself. He was compelled to creep into the sack, folding up his long, bony arms and legs, cramming his scythe in anyhow, and glowering at the soldier from the darkness of the sack with eyes set in hollows like cups. But the soldier took no notice, as he fastened the buckles of the knapsack. He knew that Death could do nothing to him now for all his glowering. He ran out of his bedroom and hugged his wife and all his children; and then he ran back for the knapsack. He carried it up to the attic at the top of his house, where apples, vegetables and herbs were stored. Reaching as high as he could, he wedged the knapsack in the angle of a roof-beam, where it was not likely to be seen, and where neither his wife nor any of his children could reach it, even if they did see it. There he left the knapsack – and Death – for fifty years.

During that fifty years, though people continued to grow older, no one, anywhere in the world, died. The soldier was happy. He had always been strong and fit, and his fifty extra years didn't stop him from looking after his farm. He saw all his children grow up and marry and have children of their own; and he saw his grandchildren grow up. He had them all to live in houses near him, and he visited, and squabbled with them, and bossed them; and he was content in the knowledge that this happy life of his would go on for ever, with his family growing ever larger around him.

But one day, as the soldier was sitting on a bench outside his house, watching his grandchildren and great-grandchildren play, an old, old woman came struggling up to his farm. She said to him, "Where is Death?"

"How would I know?" asked the soldier.

"You were dying," said the ancient woman, "but you recovered; and since that time Death has come to no one."

"Isn't that a blessing, Granny?" asked the soldier.

"For some, maybe," she said. "Not for me. Look at me. What pleasure is life for me? This body is so old. It is ugly and weak, and full of pain. I long to be dead, and to know and feel nothing – but where is Death?"

"Ah," said the soldier, who had not thought of this.

"Death has left the world," said the old woman, "but he has left behind many with mortal wounds, that cannot heal and cannot die ... And many who were drowned, and poisoned, and hanged and burned, who cannot live, and cannot die ... It was cruel of Death to leave us."

"Old woman," said the soldier, "if I knew where

Death was, I would go and call him for you."

The old woman shook her head and tutted; and grumbling, she began to drag herself away along the road, hugging her body with her arms, as if to hold herself together as she tottered and stumbled. In a couple of hours, as soon as she was out of sight, the soldier went back into his house, and climbed the stairs to the attic. He reached the knapsack down from its place on the beam. It was coated with a thick, furry layer of dust, which made him cough as he knocked it off. He carried the heavy bag down the stairs and out into the yard. He carried it a long way from his house. Then he unfastened the buckles and said, "Death; I let you go."

Death sprang from the knapsack and leapt and bounded away, his stinking old cloak flying behind him, his long, long arms and legs whirling like bones thrown in the air. He met the old woman on the road and jumped on her back, and gulped the life out of her. Her body fell dead. He ran on to the town, danced and leapt through the streets, and left few alive there. All over the world Death ran, greedily reaching for whoever was nearest to hand, the young and healthy as well as the old and sick. The graveyards filled, the cities emptied, and when, at last, Death's hunger was ended, those few left lonely and alive wandered the untended, unharvested country, searching for company. Since then, whenever there has been a plague, people have said, "Death has been fasting."

His hunger satisfied, Death returned to revenge

himself on the soldier. The soldier and his wife were now ancient, and their children were elderly, and their grandchildren looked after the farm. Still, the old soldier liked to make himself useful, and he spent one day in planting seeds in the little vegetable garden behind his house. He had the sack of seed at his feet. As he stood there, sprinkling seed and whistling, he noticed a sudden cold, a shadow, and a stink of old, damp earth. He looked up and saw Death coming for him. He picked up the sack and held it open. "Come on then, Death, come on!" he said.

Death thought the seed-sack was the knapsack and, afraid of being trapped for another fifty years, he turned and ran. The soldier frightened him so badly that Death never comes for anyone openly and honestly any more, but always creeps up so that they never see or hear him. The soldier was the last man to see Death's face.

Death did not try to catch the soldier after that; he was too afraid of him. But he took the soldier's wife, and his daughters and sons; and, one by one, his grandchildren and his great-grandchildren, and all his friends and neighbours, until there wasn't a lonelier man on all the earth than the old soldier.

"I never thought that I would live to say I was tired of living," said the soldier to himself, "but tired of it I am." And he shouted, "Come, Death! I'll go with you now. No tricks this time, I promise!" But Death was too cautious to come near the soldier again, and left him to his weary, lonely life. "Ah well, I'd better go and find him, I suppose," said the soldier.

With his knapsack on his back, he travelled from place to place, going wherever he heard there was a battle or a plague, because he knew that there he would find Death. But Death always ran away when he saw the soldier coming, and plague-cities would send out messengers to find the soldier and bring him to them, to drive the pestilence away.

The soldier was too old to travel fast, and he soon grew tired of chasing Death. The one thing he wanted was to be out of this world and at rest at last; for he was more tired of the world than anyone who has not lived so long can imagine. So he gave up chasing Death and, instead, went up to the gates of Heaven, and knocked. St. Peter opened them, with the keys in his hand.

"Please, St. Peter," said the soldier. "I know I've not kept all the commandments, but I tried. Won't you let me in, sir? I'm tired of it out here."

"Oh no," said St. Peter. "It's not that we have anything against you — but we've heard of that knapsack of yours, and we don't wish to see the inside of it." And St. Peter slammed the gates and locked them.

The soldier was determined to leave this world, one way or another, so he went next door to the Gates of Hell, and he knocked there. It was opened by one of the devils that had been in his knapsack on the blacksmith's anvil, and was still bruised from the beating.

"Please," said the soldier, "I haven't broken all the commandments, but I've tried. Won't you let me come in?"

"Let *you* in?" cried the devil. And it slammed Hell's gate and locked it.

Then the soldier tried to throw the knapsack away, for he was sure that he would be admitted to either Heaven or Hell without it; but the Devil had made sure that he could never throw it away. Whenever he tried, it would not leave his fingers.

So the soldier came back to this world, and began searching for Death once more, but Death would never wait for him. The soldier travelled so far, and through so many years, and grew so old, that he was worn away by the wind and rain until he could not be seen. Invisible, he is travelling still, with his knapsack on his back. When it is quiet, in lonely places, he can be heard sighing as he passes, and muttering to himself, "No rest. No rest. No, no rest..."

The Cloak

A pedlar once wished to travel between two towns. The road he wanted to take was long and lonely. It passed through a thick forest and had many twists and bends. At any one of them robbers might be waiting. Dozens of people had already been attacked and robbed while travelling that road, and some of them had been killed.

Nevertheless, it was a journey he had to make, and he started out early in the morning with his tall pedlar's pack strapped to his back. He could not help wondering if he would reach his destination safely.

He tramped for hours, and for many hard, rocky

miles, without meeting anyone, and although he
was hot and tired he had enough strength to thank
God that his skin was still in one piece. It was then
that he heard footsteps behind him, and the sound
of a man whistling. He could not look over his
shoulder because of his pack, so he stopped and
turned completely round. He saw a tall man,
dressed in beautiful and expensive clothes that were
all black, as if he was going to a funeral. The pedlar
was surprised he didn't have a cloak to save his fine
clothes from the weather, should it come on to rain.

The stranger saw the pedlar and called out to him,
"Good day, sir! I am glad to meet another traveller
on this road! Do you know, I've heard so many
frightful tales of robberies along here that I've been
on the point of turning back all the way. But now I
have an honest man to keep me company."

"I can't deny that I'm real glad of some company
too, sir," said the pedlar, and they went on together.

They began to talk about the weather, and how
hard and steep the road was, and then the stranger
said, "How would you like to make a deal with me,
pedlar?"

"What sort of deal?" the pedlar asked.

"You've something about you that I would like to
buy. I'll pay you a good price for it," said the
stranger.

The pedlar was a cautious man, and he cast his
eyes down while he considered what it might be that
the stranger wanted to buy from him. That was how
he noticed the stranger's neat, black shoes. The toes

were split, like the hoof of a deer, goat or sheep. They had never been made to fit human feet. The pedlar's black-clothed travelling companion was the Devil. The pedlar cried out, "It's my soul you're after!"

"No, no, no," said the Devil. "I have plenty of souls. The thing I wish to buy from you is of no use to you whatsoever. You cannot feel it, and you will not miss it – and look, I will give you all this in exchange for it." From his black coat, the Devil took a heavy purse, which he opened to show the pedlar the gold coins that crammed it.

With his eyes on the coins as he tried to count them, the pedlar asked, "What is it you want?"

"Your shadow, only your shadow. What use is it to you?"

The pedlar stopped and looked at his shadow on the road beside him. It was quite true that he could not feel it, would not miss it, and hardly ever thought about it. "Why do *you* want it?" he asked the Devil.

"That is entirely my affair," replied Lucifer. "The gold is yours. Take it."

The man held out his hand for the gold. "Have my shadow then," he said. "Quickly."

The Devil put the gold into his hand and, with a smile, stooped and lifted the man's shadow from the ground as if it were cut from black cloth like his own black clothes. He shook the shadow out and gave it a tug that tore it free of the pedlar's heels, though the pedlar felt nothing. The Devil held the shadow between his hands. In places it was so threadbare that the pedlar could see through it. He could not imagine why the Devil should want to buy such a useless thing.

"Thank you for doing business with me," said the Devil.

"Thank *you!*" said the pedlar, and he hurried on along the road with his gold, as glad to leave his travelling companion as he had been to meet him.

The Devil watched until the pedlar was out of sight, and then he spread the shadow and drew it round his shoulders like a cloak. The Devil vanished in the deep shadow that fell across the road.

The pedlar trudged on, with a great fear of what he had done, for dealing with the Devil never came to any good. But the next morning he found that the gold coins had not changed into leaves or ashes, as he had feared they would, and he felt happier. He began to plan the best way to use the gold to ensure his future comfort.

He planned well. He invested his gold and looked after the profit it brought him. He became rich, and he bought land, and houses, and became richer. He soon had no need to worry about what might become of his children or himself in the years to come. And yet he behaved so oddly that his neighbours thought him mad. He stayed in his house all day long, shutting himself up in a darkened room, and went out only at night. Even his friends and children could not coax him from his frowsty room into another if sunlight was shining through the windows. He feared sunlight, and would not put even his fingertip or the toe of his shoe into it.

"Who knows why?" said some wit of the town. "Perhaps he casts no shadow!"

When the old pedlar heard this remark being repeated beneath the shuttered windows of his dim room, he flinched and looked most carefully all about him, his anxious eyes searching for a shadow in the shadows. For though it was true that he cast no shadow, his shadow was still with him – and the Devil was wrapped in it.

The Miserly Ghost

There was an Icelandic farmhouse that was haunted. The farmer and his wife were forced to keep one of the bedrooms locked because, at night, eerie and frightening noises were heard coming from it. All night long there would be moans and wailing cries, and a continual clattering, rattling sound. The farmer and his wife were used to this, and it never disturbed them, but guests in other bedrooms rarely had a good night's sleep. Few people were prepared to spend a night in that house, and this grieved the farmer's wife, for she liked visitors. She was also sorry that such a fine big room had to be locked. When she was in there, polishing and sweeping during the day, she often admired it, and she would have liked it for her own bedroom, if only the ghost could have been laid. It didn't seem likely that it ever would be, though, because people who had tried to lay it had been found the next day, lying in the big bed in the haunted room, black and blue and struck dead. Now there didn't seem to be anyone left who wanted to try to deal with that ghost.

Late one evening an old beggar-woman came to the farm, asking for food. The farm-wife took her into the kitchen and gave her some porridge. While she was eating, the old beggar asked if there was somewhere about the farm she might sleep, out of the wet and the cold. "There's a grand big room upstairs, with a bed, a carpet, curtains and all," said the farm-wife. "You can sleep there if you don't mind sharing with the ghost."

"Oh yes, I'll do that," said the old beggar-woman. "I know a trick worth a ghost or two."

Then the farm-wife was alarmed and explained that she had only been joking. She told the old woman how people had been killed by the ghost in that room, and how it was always kept locked, but the old woman wouldn't listen. "Just tell me how to find the room, and give me the key," she said, "and you get off to your own bed. Don't worry about me." Eventually the farm-wife decided that if the old woman was so determined to spend the night with the ghost, she would let her. She handed over the key to the haunted room and went up to bed, leaving the old beggar sitting by the kitchen fire.

The old woman waited until everyone in the farmhouse was asleep, and then she let herself out of the kitchen-door and ran to the graveyard, which wasn't far away. There she found a new grave, and she lay down in the mud on the top of it, and rolled about until all her clothes, and her hair and face, were covered with grave-mould. She also took off one of her woollen gloves and dragged it through the cold, wet grass. Then she went back to the farmhouse.

The candle that the farm-wife had left for her was still burning. Holding it, she lit her way up the steep, dark stairs to the door of the haunted room. She unlocked the door and went in, and stopped in admiration, for it was indeed a large, splendid room. There was a big fireplace to warm it, and velvet curtains at the window, a flowered carpet on the floor, and a big, soft bed with many blankets and pillows. The old woman climbed into the bed with all her muddy clothes on, put her candle on the side-table, and blew the flame out. In the quiet darkness she snuggled down and made herself comfortable. It had been a long, long time since she had slept in a bed and she was determined to enjoy that night.

For a while she dozed, but was woken by the sound of the bedroom door opening. Then she came wide awake, and made sure that the hand wearing the cold, wet glove was on top of the blankets. Lying very still, she turned her eyes to the side and saw, in the darkness, a something poke its head round the door. The something looked all round the room. Then it spoke. "It's nice and clean in here," it said.

It came right into the room then and, seeing someone in the bed, came to see what was there. The old woman shut her eyes and held her breath. The ghost stood over her, and it smelt the grave-mould that covered her. That made it think that she was dead, like itself. Just to make sure, it touched the hand that lay out on the blankets wearing the cold, wet glove that the old woman had dragged through the grass in the graveyard. The ghost thought that it was a cold, dead hand, and it was certain that the old woman was dead. After that it took no more notice of her.

The old woman carefully opened one eye, and saw the ghost go to the foot of the bed, where it stooped over something. She did not care what. Now, she thought, she could leave the ghost to its own affairs, and settle herself down to a really good night's sleep in the big bed. She turned on her side, pushed her head into the pillow, and began to drift off into a deep sleep.

The ghost, at the foot of the bed, pulled up some floorboards and threw them aside with a crash. The old woman jumped with fright, and sat up, staring round. She saw the ghost standing at the foot of the bed, quiet again, and she lay down, grumbling, but determined that, from now on, she would ignore any noise the ghost made, and go to sleep.

The ghost bent down and reached into the space

beneath the floorboards. It gathered into its arms dozens and dozens of gold coins and tossed them all into the air, so they would fall about its head. They hit the floor and chinked and rattled; and they rolled into corners, and spun round and round and round, a long-drawn-out and loud sound in the quiet night. Then, just when the old woman thought that all the noise was over, the ghost gave a soft laugh. The old woman sighed to herself. Still, never mind, she thought. Perhaps now it will go away.

But, when all the coins had fallen, and had finished rolling and spinning, the ghost gathered them all up again, and threw them into the air a second time. They struck the ceiling, made startling noises against the glass in the window; chinked together, clunked on the floor, rolled and span with long rattles.

The old woman pulled a pillow over her head. It did nothing to muffle the sound of the ghost scampering over the floor and giggling as it collected up its coins for another throw. This time, as it tossed the coins into the air, it cried loudly, "Wheeee!" The sounds of the coins clattering and rattling on the floor were as loud as ever.

The old woman thought that she would wait until the ghost got tired but, being a ghost, it didn't get tired. Hours later, the old woman was still lying awake, with her arms folded, listening to the excited cries of the ghost, and to the coins falling to the floor. She decided that she couldn't bear it any longer. She got out of the bed, pulled the blankets from it, and left the house. She went to the churchyard, looked about until she saw the open grave the ghost had left, and climbed into it, wrapping herself in the blankets. "*Now*," she said, "I shall get some sleep."

She had an hour's sleep, and then it was dawn, and the ghost came back to its grave. There lay the old woman in it. The ghost was furious, and screamed and threw stones about until the old woman woke. "Back already?" she said. "Go and play with your pennies for another hour, will you, and let me sleep."

"If daylight catches me out of my grave, I shall be destroyed!" cried the ghost. "Out! Out!"

The old woman moaned and sat up. "I'll get out and let you in," she said, "if you'll swear to me, by your grave, that you'll never leave it again."

"What? Never see my gold again?"

"If you hadn't loved your gold so much when you were alive, you wouldn't be so tied to it now," said the old woman. "Swear, or stay out there and be destroyed; it's all one to me."

The ghost saw that it was beaten, and it swore, by its grave, that it would never come out at night to play with its treasure again. "Now hurry and get out," it begged the old woman. "It's almost day."

The old woman climbed slowly out of the grave. "You'll be happier, you know," she said. "Under the earth's the place for the dead. Up on top's for the living."

But the ghost had jumped into its grave and

pulled the earth over itself. The grave looked as neat as if it had never been opened.

The old woman went back to the farmhouse and stirred up the kitchen-fire. She was sitting by it when the farm-wife came down, and the old beggar-woman told her all that had happened during the night. Then she went back to bed and slept until evening.

When the old woman got up at last, she found the farmer and his wife in a good mood. The farmer had fetched the gold that the old miser had hidden under the floorboards, and there was a fortune. The farmer and his wife insisted that the old woman took a share, which she was glad to do; and her share was so much that she was able to set herself up in a little house nearby, instead of begging from farm to farm.

However, after it was discovered what a muddy mess she had made of their best bed, she did not remain on good terms with the farmer and his wife.

Tom Otter

A man was once brought before a King and accused of murdering the King's wisest adviser. "What is your name?" the King asked.

"Tom Otter," the man replied.

"And are you guilty of this crime, Tom Otter?"

"I am guilty," said Tom Otter. "I lay in wait for your adviser, and when he came by, I stabbed him to death – but hear my reasons for doing so."

"Tell them," said the King.

"This man always gave you good counsel, that turned out well for you, King, and so you thought highly of him; but to those of your subjects who are not rich and powerful he was a wicked man. He wanted my father's land, but my father would not sell. So this adviser of yours paid men to wait – as I waited – and when my father and brother came by, they murdered them both. Then from my mother, the widow, he bought the land cheaply. That is why I murdered your adviser. If I took one life from him, then he took two from me; so give me the life I am owed, King, and let me go free."

The King considered. He knew that the story Tom Otter told was true – but he also knew that the widow and sons of his dead adviser wanted Tom Otter executed. "This is my decision," said the King. "You are eloquent, Tom Otter, but is your eloquence equal to saving your life? You shall have a day's reprieve. If, at the end of that time, you can ask a riddle which neither I, nor any man or woman here, can answer, then I shall pardon you. But if your riddle can be answered within three days, then you will be hanged."

The King was certain that no man under sentence of death could, in a single day, make a riddle that all the sharpest minds of his court could not solve. And so Tom Otter would be executed, but the King would have seemed to have been merciful.

Tom Otter was taken to a cell and locked in for a day and a night. He thought of every riddle he knew, and all were too easy. He tried to invent new riddles, but no words would come. At dawn, he hauled himself up to the cell window, to see the sky while he could; and what he saw through the cell window gave him hope.

The jailers soon came to unlock his cell and take him to the court. "Have you made a riddle?" the King asked.

Tom Otter looked round at the watching faces of the cleverest people in the land, all assembled there to judge him and hang him, and he said, "I have, King, and this is my riddle:

'There were five tongues within one head,
The sixth went out to seek for bread,
To feed the living within the dead.
Fearful I went, but bold I come in,
For from the dead I've seen the living spring.
Blessed may all the good gods be,
For the six have set the seventh free!'

Now, King, lords, ladies – tell me what this might be."

The King looked about him at his advisers, who soon began to scowl, and to bite their lips and thumbs, as they tried to think of something which the rhyme might be describing. After an hour or so, they asked if they could retire, and they were led to small, quiet rooms, hung with green cloth, where quiet music was played to help them think. Tom Otter was led back to his cell.

At the end of the three days they and Tom Otter were brought back into the court-room.

"Now, gentlemen, ladies," said the King. "Let us have your answers."

There was silence.

"Come, people," said the King. "You must have some answer."

But all the advisers, to their shame, had to admit that they had been unable to think of an answer which fitted all the parts of the riddle.

"It seems that my riddle cannot be answered, King," Tom Otter called out. "Remember your promise."

"I gave my word that you should be freed, and you are," said the King. "But tell us now; what is the answer to the riddle?"

"Your justice, King," Tom Otter answered; and there rose a great muttering and outcry from the advisers.

"Justice?" said the King. "That does not answer the riddle. What do you mean?"

"I mean, King, that if you look to your justice, you may find the riddle's answer." Tom Otter would say no more than that, but hastily left the court.

Outside friends were waiting for him, with fast horses and weapons, but before he would leave, Tom Otter pointed out to them the window of the cell he had been imprisoned in; and then he pointed out the body of an executed man which hung from the castle walls opposite the cell window. "Take off your hats to that gentleman," Tom Otter said. "He saved my life."

His friends were bewildered, but they took off their hats and, as they looked up at the corpse, they saw a surprising thing. Into the body's gaping mouth flew a bird. After a second, out it flew again. A bird had built its nest, and was feeding its chicks, inside the dead man's mouth.

Then Tom Otter's friends escorted him to the coast, where he took ship for a foreign land. He never came back.

The Moon

A long, long time ago, a little time after the Beginning of All Things, but not long after, there was a sun to shine in the sky by day, but no light at all by night, except for the weak and flickering light of fires and candles. At midnight the darkness was vast, unending, over all the earth, and no firelight could pierce it. So the people of the earth employed four witches of great skill to make a lamp to light the earth when it was dark. The four witches talked together, and planned, and made a large, flat, thin disc of silver. With their magic art they filled it with light from the sun, and it shone brightly, but they could not make it shine as brightly or warmly as the sun. They hung this disc from the tallest tree that grew on top of the highest mountain, and they called it "the Moon". By day the sun outshone it, and it could not be seen; but every night its shining lit the whole earth.

And now night was a busy time. By the moon's radiance husbands, wives and sweethearts were unfaithful; goods were stolen, travellers robbed, game poached; barns, haystacks and houses fired; and every possible sin committed; for the wonderful new moon gave light enough for the sinners to see what they were doing, but not enough light for them to be recognized.

In time one of the witches who had made the moon died, demanding in his last words that his quarter of the moon should be buried with him. So the other three witches climbed the mountain, took down the moon, and cut a quarter from it, which they buried with their dead comrade.

Within a week another of the witches died, and she too wanted her quarter of the moon buried with her; and it was. And within the next two weeks, the other two witches died, and the last two quarters of the moon were buried with them. The old impenetrable darkness returned to the earth at night; and the people, who had been delighting in all sorts of cheating and wickedness, were forced to seem much better than they were, for lack of light. There was no one left above the ground capable of making another moon.

All four quarters of the moon were now in the

Underworld, and they continued to shine down there, where the dead lay in their graveclothes, waiting for Judgement Day. Down there, where there had been darkness for eternity, the cold shining of the moon seemed as fierce and hot as that of the sun. The dead began to wake. They stirred, opened their sunken eyes, and sat up, thinking that the Day of Judgement had come.

But when the earth above them did not split open, when there came no blowing of horns, no glory, no visions of Heaven, they looked about for the source of the light that had woken them. They found the four quarters of the moon and fitted them together. The new light in the Underworld grew brighter still.

The light was so strong that the dead could not sleep. They hung the moon from the Underworld's roof, and by its light they began a new life. They cut the roots of plants and brewed liquor from them. They married among themselves and set up households under the earth. They took up business, each practising the craft they had followed in life. They got drunk on their root-beer and they stamped, shouted, sang and danced, skeleton with cadaver.

All night long, and all day long too, the people on earth above could hear the sound of hammering beneath their feet, the sound of sawing, and loud talking; of shooting and shouting and, even worse, of drunken singing and arguing. These disturbing sounds never stopped, for though darkness ended the day on earth, the moon shone steadily, without interruption, in the Underworld. When graves were dug for those who died above ground, the living looked down into the Underworld and saw light shining eerily from a hole at their feet. They spied on the hustle and bustle of trade and pleasure in the Land of the Dead. As people died on earth, the population of the Underworld grew, and the infernal, underground din grew louder and louder.

At last the woken dead were so many, and became so drunk, and made so much uproar with their fighting, singing and dancing, that St. Peter heard them as he went to lock the gates of Heaven. He was not sure what the row could be, so he leaned out of the gates and cocked his head and listened; and the noise was so terrible that he thought the Devil had broken free of the chains with which the Archangel Michael had bound him, and was rallying the hosts of Hell before attacking Heaven itself.

This conclusion threw St. Peter into a panic and, leaving the gates of Paradise unlocked and open wide, he ran to one of Heaven's many mansions, the home of the Archangel Michael, Captain of the Hosts of Heaven.

"To arms, Michael!" he cried. "Judgement is here! The Devil has broken loose and is coming upon us! Save us! Arm! Defend Paradise!"

The Archangel rose at once and, while horns were blown throughout Heaven to summon his army of angels, he put on his armour, which was hammered out of stars and glared with a million intensities of blue, white, red and green light. He drew over his head the helmet, plumed with comet's tails; cinched tight about his waist the black sword-belt with its brilliant sword; and took up his lance which was a single, long, fiercely barbed sunbeam. He left his hall and mounted his eight-legged dragon-horse and rode, at the head of his host, down the Milky Way to earth.

The angels kicked their horses to the gallop as they neared the earth, and the roar of their hooves echoed over the world and terrified the living who listened to it in their darkness, awestruck. Glaring light flashed and leapt over the whole sky, and the frightened people thought they saw glimpses of giant figures in these fearful lightning flashes.

At Michael's word of command, the earth opened, and the Angelic Host entered the Underworld. A wild, agonized cry burst from the dead there, and ran and echoed and re-echoed through all the caverns underground; for if the light that shone from the moon was as bright as the sun to their spent eyes, then the light that burned from the angels' armour, that flared from their helmets' plumes, that blazed goldenly from Michael's lance, caused them more anguish than if a living man should look directly into the light of three suns. Already the weaker of them were sinking down, withering and returning to their former sleep.

Then the Archangel Michael drew his sword and held it high above his head. It sang out high and loudly in praise of God, and ignited with an incandescent white fire: an undying lightning-flash. The sword left no darkness, no shadows, anywhere in the Underworld. An unrelieved, remorseless light washed the dimness from every hollow and every corner, made everything flat and distanceless. Nothing human, living or dead, could withstand that radiance. "Sleep!" Michael shouted, in a voice that reached as far as the light from his sword. "Sleep!" Now the strongest of the dead fell before his command, crumbled, faded, and slept.

The Archangel sheathed his sword, and the full glare of the light dimmed. Michael kicked up his dragon-horse and rode on into Hell itself, where he found the Devil chained, as he had left him. So he knew that it had not been the Devil who had woken the dead. Back he rode to the Underworld, and began the search for the cause of the dead's awakening. In all the shimmer of light from the angels' armour, it was not easy to see the moon, but at last Michael saw it, put up his lance, and hooked down the moon on its tip. He slung the moon over his shoulder and led his troops out of the Underworld.

While his troopers rode up the Milky Way to Heaven, the Archangel rode out across the dark sky, and hung the moon on the fortress walls of God's Citadel, where it has hung ever since. The Archangel was careful to hang it so high that it could never again be reached from any tree or mountain top on earth.

But with the moon set so high in the sky, it again

lit the whole world, and shone with unfailing brightness every single night. Soon all the people of the world were using its light to aid them in committing their crimes, both large and small. Their neighbours did not know who the sinners were, but God did, and He was angry.

He wanted to take the moon down from the sky, so there would be less opportunity for His people to sin; but St. Peter and St. Paul pointed out that the moon was useful to many innocent people: to travellers, watchmen, shepherds, to nurses who must sit with the sick, to sailors, and those who must carry urgent news. So God agreed that the moon might remain in the sky, but decreed that it was not to shine every night; and St. Peter was given the job of regulating the light of the moon, turning it up and down, so that it only shines with its full light for a few nights each month, to give fewer chances of devilry to the people of the earth.

But if God had really wanted to prevent His people sinning, He would have done better to have taken down both the sun and moon from the sky, and left us to blunder in perpetual darkness; and even then Hell would have been more crowded than Heaven.

The Bishop of the Butterfly

In the time of King John there lived a man named Peter des Roches, who was the Bishop of Winchester. He preached a religion that praised poverty, but he was a rich man himself. He owned much land, and he loved to hunt over it. Riding one day in pursuit of a red deer, he drove his horse so hard that he left the other hunters behind. Yet he came no nearer to the deer and hounds.

He rode into a sweet-scented but chill fog. When it cleared and he could see again, nothing had changed, or so it seemed. He was in the forest, as before, but everything was silent. There was not the slightest breeze, so there were no sounds of leaves and branches rubbing and rustling against each other. And he could hear no noise of hooves, or men's voices, or hounds baying, or even birdsong. It seemed that, suddenly, only the Bishop and his horse were alive in the whole world.

The Bishop rode on slowly through the silent forest. No hunters overtook him. He came upon none of his hounds, or the stag, or any other creature. But then he saw the towers and walls of a castle through the trees, a high, strong, stone castle that had not been there the day before. The Bishop reined in his horse and sat looking at the castle, astonished and afraid. Then he put himself under the protection of his god, and rode on.

The bridge of the castle was down, and a small door in the great door open. The keeper of this door called out and asked the Bishop who he was, and what he wanted.

The Bishop wondered at being asked this in his own forest, but he replied, "Peter des Roches, a man of God, and the Bishop of Winchester . . . But who is the master of this castle?"

"A greater man than you," answered the door-keeper.

"Indeed? And would it be possible to speak with him?" asked the Bishop.

"It will. We last had a visit from the world two centuries ago," said the door-keeper.

The Bishop rode over the bridge into the castle, and a man came to take his horse, while others came out of the castle to escort him inside. He looked at their strange clothes and their stiff, white faces, and his body was filled with fear, and his mind with curiosity and wonder.

He was led through long, cold corridors of stone to a high hall, where one whole wall was covered with a banner showing a black raven on a red ground. In the centre of the hall there was a strange thing – a massive table, circular in shape, like no other table the Bishop had ever seen, with many fine big chairs set round it.

At the end of the hall a man sat beside a small table on which was placed a chessboard. He was the biggest man the Bishop had ever seen, a giant of seven feet tall or more, with long moustachioes, a long beard, and a stiff crest of hair. "Peter des Roches," said the giant, "you are welcome if you play chess!"

"Then I am welcome," said the Bishop. Seating himself on the other side of the table, he began the game. It was a long game, and the Bishop lost. The giant suggested another game, which he won in a few minutes; and then a third which he won in an hour. "You are unlikely to beat me at this, or any other game, Bishop," said the giant. "In my life I was the most cunning schemer, the greatest warrior, and the finest chess-player in the land; and since that time I have had seven hundred years to practise all my skills."

"My Lord," said the Bishop, "I guess that you were a King, but may I, without giving offence, ask your name?"

"In life my name was Arthur ap Uther, Pendragon, King of the Britons. Am I forgotten on earth?"

"No," said the Bishop simply, though his heart almost stopped beating within him. "You are not forgotten, Pendragon; but it was thought that, long since, you would have found your place in Heaven."

"Ah, my life did not fit me for that," said Arthur. "I am too foul a sinner for Heaven."

"Then – forgive me, Pendragon – but why are you not in Hell?"

"Why, my courage was too great, my ambition too high, my fame too glorious, to be doused in Hell. So here I wait, and must wait, until the world is folded up and brought to an end. Then, on Judgement Day, my trial will be heard. All the wrong I did will be weighed against the good, and all those I harmed shall speak against all those who have loved and been inspired by my name. At the very end the decision will be given, and I shall either captain Michael's army, or be thrown into Hell's darkness. I cannot tell or hope which; I can only wait; and a long, tiresome wait it has been and is still to be, Lord Bishop! Will you play another game?"

So the Bishop and the King played another game of chess, and the Bishop lost. Then they went to the Round Table, where the Bishop sat amongst the famous knights, and entertained them by telling all he could remember of the happenings in the world since they had last had a living guest. After the meal was finished, the King asked the Bishop if he would stay with them for a while, but the Bishop begged to be allowed to leave. He knew that he had somehow left his own world for another, and that for every minute he spent with Arthur and his knights, a year might be passing on earth.

"You must understand, Pendragon," he said, "that I am afraid for my own silly soul – for if the time slips away and I come to Judgement in the company of King Arthur, might I not be overlooked?"

Arthur laughed, and said that he might leave.

"Yet when I join my huntsmen again, and tell them where I have been, what will they say to me? Tell me, how am I to prove that I have played chess and eaten meat with Arthur ap Uther, Pendragon, King of the Britons?"

"Raise your right hand and clench it into a fist," said Arthur, and the Bishop did so. "Now open your hand." The Bishop opened his fist, and from his palm flew a living butterfly, bright and quick. "This is your proof, for those who doubt you," said Arthur. "It shall never fail, till your life's end."

The Bishop bowed and thanked him, and went out into the courtyard, where he mounted his horse and rode through the castle gate. He rode into the silent forest, where no bird or animal moved, and into a scented, cold fog, which quickly cleared. Then he heard the sound of horses' hooves, and his fellow-huntsmen rode past, following the hounds and calling to him.

When he told his story that evening, no one

would call him a liar because he was a Bishop, but no one believed him either. He clenched his fist, opened it, and released a butterfly. Everyone saw it, and no one would believe that it came from his hand. Not until he had clenched and opened his fist ten times, and there were ten butterflies, of blue and tawny and yellow and red, bobbing through the air was anyone convinced.

This strange power remained with Peter des Roches all his life, and he became known as "The Bishop of the Butterfly". People travelled to him from all over England, and asked for a butterfly from his hand, as a benediction.

Fires in the Graveyard

A soldier had been fighting for his Emperor for many months and was given leave to visit his family. Instead of going straight home, he stopped off to visit a friend, and settled down by the fire to eat, talk and drink with him.

"You'll be wanting the news," his friend said. "Did you know the witch is dead?"

"What? The old witch dead and gone?" said the soldier. "I thought he would never die."

"He's dead right enough," said his friend, "but whether he's gone, that's another matter."

When the soldier got up to leave it was dark

outside and his friend asked him to stay the night. "You never know what you might meet out there, and you have to pass the graveyard," he said. But the soldier felt guilty at having visited his friend before his family, and he was determined to go home now. "Nothing will dare to hurt me," he said. "Remember; a soldier is the property of the Emperor – even ghosts and ghouls know that!" And he marched off into the dark.

His journey was uneventful until he reached the graveyard, and then he saw, through the bushes and tombstones, the flickering, flaring light of a fire. The soldier could not think why a fire should be burning in the graveyard at that time of night. He stood puzzling for a while, and then he turned in at the graveyard gate.

He followed the path and came to the wide yellow circle of light made by the fire. Sitting in the middle of the fire was the witch who had died. He was sitting cross-legged among the flames, sewing the seams of a boot.

"Hello, Master, how are you?" asked the soldier. "You look well."

The witch looked down at him from the fire. "I wish you a good night, trooper. Thank you for your enquiry; I never felt better. I'm just off to a wedding in the village. Would you like to come along with me?"

"Oh yes, I never pass up a chance to enjoy myself," said the soldier. "There's little enough pleasure in this world."

The witch put on the boots he had just finished sewing, and climbed down from the bonfire. "Let's go together then."

They walked to the village, and came to a house where a noisy wedding celebration was going on, with singing, dancing and drinking. The soldier and the witch went into the house together. The witch was polite to all present, and the wedding-guests were even more polite to the witch than they had been while he was alive. They offered him a share of all the food and drink they had, and he courteously touched them to his lips, though he remarked to the soldier that he had no need for such things now. After a while the witch began to make patterns in the air with his hands, and everyone except the soldier fell asleep. The soldier felt drowsy, but he kept his eyes open, and he saw what happened. The witch took from his pocket two glass phials and a sharp cobbler's awl. He went up to the bride and groom, stabbed the groom's hand with the awl, and drew off some of his blood into one of the phials. He stoppered it, and put it away in his pocket. Then he drew off some of the bride's blood, in the same way, into the second phial; and he stoppered that and put it into the other pocket. He called good-night to everyone, though they were all asleep, and left the house. The soldier roused himself and followed, hurrying down the street after the witch.

"Master!" he shouted. "Tell me; why did you take their blood like that?"

"Oh, you saw that, did you?" said the witch. "To kill them. Why else?"

"You mean they'll die, those two poor young people?"

"Tomorrow morning they won't wake. No one will be able to wake them because no one knows how to break my spell. There isn't another witch within a thousand miles skilful enough to do it."

"You must be skilful indeed," said the soldier. "I do admire cleverness. Brains, that's the most admirable part of a man, and you must have plenty ... How is it done?"

"Quite simply," answered the witch, "but it's knowing how. I have the groom's blood in my left-hand pocket, the bride's in my right, and to restore them, all I would have to do is make a slit in their heels and pour the blood back into them. They would recover at once."

"Amazing!" said the soldier. "What else can you do?"

"Anything I choose. I could turn myself into any kind of bird or animal, or even an insect. I can raise or quell a storm, turn stones into diamonds, cats into ladies, foxes into men – why, you can see for yourself that not even death bothers me."

"It is humbling to walk beside you, sir," said the soldier. "You are a great man. It's clear to me that no one could even hope to defeat you."

"True, no one could. They would have to make a pyre of one hundred bundles of aspen boughs, and each bundle would have to contain a hundred boughs. They would have to take me from my grave at mid-day and throw me on the pyre, and set light to it, and even then they would have no chance of defeating me, for from my burning body would come every kind of creature, flying, crawling and running, and if even one of them, one fly or one little maggot, were to escape, I should escape in it." As he finished saying this they reached the ashes of the witch's fire, and his open grave, and the witch turned to the soldier and said, "It has been so pleasant talking to you like this, but now I must tear you to pieces."

"What?" said the soldier.

"If I let you go, you would tell all this, and people will be pestering me with attempts to destroy me," said the witch and, drawing back his lips from his long, sharp teeth, he leapt at the soldier, who drew his sword and began a desperate fight. Luckily for him, it was not long before dawn, and he was still keeping the witch at sword's length when the first light of the sun sent the ghost back into its grave.

Very weary, the soldier trudged back into the village, where he went from house to house, banging on doors and shouting until he had everyone awake. Many people were glad to see him, but alarmed by his appearance. They asked had he travelled all night, had he fought with robbers, was he ill?

"No time for that," said the soldier. "There are two still asleep. Where are the bride and groom who were married yesterday?"

And then it was found that the bride and groom could not be wakened; and the people were puzzled to know how the soldier had known about the wedding; while others said they had *thought* they'd seen him there ... The soldier said, "I know how to cure them. Listen to what I tell you. I am tired, and I am going to stay here, but some of you must go to the graveyard and dig up the witch. There are phials of blood in his pockets. Bring them here. Others of you must collect ten thousand aspen boughs and make them into a hundred bundles of a hundred boughs each; and then you must make them into a funeral pyre. You must do all this before mid-day, so hurry."

Two men set out at once, to the graveyard, to dig up the witch, while every man, woman and child in the village hunted for aspen boughs. The soldier went to bed.

An hour before mid-day they wakened him. The aspen-boughs had been gathered, the pyre built. The witch lay on it, waiting.

"Everyone must take a weapon," said the soldier. "A club, a stick, an axe, a hoe, a knife, arrows, pistols, anything – and we must all stand round the pyre, circle after circle of us. As the witch burns, his spirit will attempt to escape in a thousand different shapes. We must kill them all. If even one little fly escapes, he will escape to torment and murder us."

So everyone took tools and weapons and followed the soldier to the graveyard. The wood of the pyre was set alight, and the villagers stood round in circle after circle. As the witch's body began to burn, a flock of crows burst upwards from the flames. Arrows and bullets shot them down. Spiders scurried from the bottom of the pyre. Feet trampled and stamped on them. Hoes and spades chopped worms and maggots and lizards. Children swotted flies and mice with brooms. Every crawling, flying, slithering, running thing that tried to leave the pyre was killed, or thrown back into the flames. When all was burned to ashes, the soldier had them scattered and blown away.

"Now," he said, "where are the phials of blood from his pockets?"

The phials were given to him, and everyone followed the soldier back to the village, to the house of the bride and groom, who still lay on their bed like dead people.

"Which phial came from his left pocket and which from his right?" the soldier asked.

No one knew.

"Oh well, blood is blood," said the soldier, and he slit the heels of the bride and groom and poured the contents of a phial into each of them. Immediately they awoke and sat up, and the whole village was delighted and declared the soldier a hero. For the duration of his leave he was waited on, and fed, and toasted, and never had to buy a drink.

Later, when the soldier had gone back to his regiment, the behaviour of the newly-married couple made people say that the soldier should have been more particular about which phial he poured into which heel. But everyone is allowed one mistake.

The Errand

There was once a widow who had one son and one daughter, and she loved them both.

The daughter was courted by a merchant from a distant land who wanted to marry her and take her to live with him. The widow would not hear of it, because she could not bear to lose her daughter.

"Mother," said her son, "let my sister marry the man she loves, and I promise you that if you ever need her, I will travel to her husband's house and bring her back to you."

And, on this condition, the widow gave her permission for the marriage to take place.

The daughter went away to live in her husband's

land, and there she was happy. She was visited, sometimes, by her mother and brother, and sometimes she visited them; and many letters and presents made the long journey between them.

One night the young woman was sitting by her parlour fire, reading. The clock had just struck midnight, but the story she read was so good that she lit another candle and read on. She was startled by a tapping at the window, and the sound of her name being called. She went to the window and looked out, and there stood her brother. He stared so fixedly at her, and seemed so pale that she thought he must be ill. She opened the window and said, "Brother, what is the matter? Why are you here so late? Why didn't you write to me – why have you come?"

"Come," he said.

The girl could only think that her mother and brother had been on their way to visit her and there had been an accident. She thought of her mother stranded somewhere near in the night, perhaps hurt, and she put a shawl about her shoulders and ran out of the house. Putting her hand into her brother's, she said, "Let us go to our mother."

Her brother's hand was cold as ice-water, and closed about hers with the tightest grip she had ever felt. He started away immediately, leading her along the road. They walked slowly, and yet the hills and trees slipped past as though they were flying. The woman could not be sure if they were really travelling so fast, or if it was only the effect of the clouds covering and uncovering the moon. They seemed to float on the moonlight and shadows like a light boat on swift water.

They came to a river and skimmed the trees and water shadows beside it. The young woman listened for a while to the sound of the river, and she said, "It's strange, but I hear words from the water, and it seems to be saying, 'See the living walk with the dead.'"

"You are in bed and dreaming," said her brother.

She laughed and said, "Perhaps I am."

They drifted on and passed beneath trees that arched high over the road, and made the moonlight shiver as the breeze shook their leaves. "Listen," said the young woman. "I hear the leaves speaking. They are saying, 'See the dead lead the living.'"

"You are asleep and dreaming," her brother repeated.

"I think I may be," she said.

On they went, the shadows flowing round them and growing more faint as morning approached. The young woman thought that she recognized the dimly seen hills as the hills of her native country, though she knew that she could not have come so far in a single night. All round them the birds began to wake and twitter, and she exclaimed, "Listen! I hear the birds talking, and they are saying, 'See the living and the dead.'"

"You are asleep and dreaming," said her brother.

"I think I am," she said, as the day dawned, and she saw before her the city where she had been born.

Her brother led her through the streets, through tunnels of brick walls. The windows shone in the first cold light, and all the birds sang. The bells of every church in the city were ringing, as they do for a death. The young woman was sure that she was dreaming – a bad dream, for on the door of house after house she saw painted the red cross that meant plague.

In her dream they reached the door of their mother's house, and the young woman turned to her brother. She saw that his face was thinned to the bone, and wretchedly pale. Before she could speak, he said, "Go in to our mother. Tell her I loved her, and that I kept my promise."

A cockerel crowed loudly, and her brother's hand melted from hers. He vanished like a shadow in light – and she knew then why her mother needed her.

The Dog and the Ghost

There was once a man who went poaching for hares and rabbits, and took his dog with him. He went a long way, stopped for a drink, and by the time he had walked half-way home again, it was dark.

On his way he had to pass a graveyard and, as he approached the cemetery gates, he was appalled to see a tall figure wrapped in white cloths drift through the gates and into the road. It stopped, facing him and waiting. The man was sure that it was a ghost, and that it was going to attack him. He didn't know what to do, because he had to go past it to get home. After a long time of hesitating, he began to say the Lord's Prayer out loud, in a shaking voice, and walked straight on.

The prayer didn't discourage the ghost. As the man drew near to it, it stretched out long armbones from its shroud and grabbed him. Its fingerbones dug deep into his flesh. The dog, growling, with all its hair on end, locked its teeth between the bones of the ghost's legs. The ghost howled, such a noise that the man's flesh turned cold and he shuddered violently. The ghost howled again, and tried to shake the dog off, but the dog hung on, though it was dragged along the ground and jerked in the air. It was determined to save its master. Seeing that the ghost's attention was distracted, the man lifted up his feet and ran away hard, ran all the way home. He went shaking to bed.

The dog and the ghost fought all night, until the dawn came and the ghost went gibbering and limping to its grave. The dog ran home and lay down at the door of its master's house. There its mistress found it the next morning, and patted its head as she went by. The children came out, gave the dog its breakfast, and stroked it. The old granny came out and gave it a titbit. But when its master came out, the dog leapt on him, knocked him down, snarling and slavering, and tried to bite out his throat. If people hadn't run up with sticks and beaten the animal off, it would have killed him. The moment it had the chance, the dog rushed at him again, and again tried to savage him.

"What's the matter with it?" people asked. "It used to be a good dog. Has it gone mad?"

Then the man told them about his adventure with

the ghost, and how the dog had loved him enough the night before to save him from it. "But it was still fighting with the ghost when I ran away," he said. "Can the ghost somehow have bewitched it?"

"Bewitched!" said the man's old mother. "If you want to know why the dog attacked you just now, it's simple enough. It risked its life for you last night, and you are so despicable that you ran away to your safe, warm bed, and left it to fight the ghost. No wonder it's angry with you! I wouldn't wonder if it holds this grudge against you for the rest of its life."

And this was true. Every time the dog got the chance, it savagely attacked its master and in the end it had to be sold to another man who lived a long way off. The dog's old master was careful never to go poaching in that direction until he heard that the animal was dead... And he never stayed out late enough to see the ghost again either.

Where Neither Age Nor Death Is

There was once a King who had twin sons. They were raised together from birth, schooled together, trained together. They ate, played and slept together, and had never spent an hour apart. But when they had grown to young men, a plague came to the city. Both princes fell ill. The elder recovered, and the younger died.

The surviving brother despaired. He could not understand that he would never see his brother again. His grief was painful, and he could see no end to it. "Now I know, and I feel, that I shall die too," he said. "It is as if my life is a small, small room, and

Death is standing at the only door." He went to his father and said, "I cannot stay here with you any longer, for in this place there is only Death, whether it comes quickly, or slowly with Age. I am going to leave and search for a place where neither Age nor Death is. Only in that place can I rest and be happy."

The King was sad to see him go, and feared for him, but he knew how great was his son's grief, and did not try to stop him. The Prince took little with him and said goodbye to no one. He mounted his horse, and set out on his long journey to discover the land where neither Age nor Death is.

He rode through all the countries of the world, but in all of them he saw Age and Death, and had to go on searching. At last he came to the edge of an immense lake, whose further shore could not be seen. A woman was dipping water from the lake in a sieve. Most of the water ran back through the sieve into the lake again, but a few droplets remained, which she scattered on the ground. When she saw the Prince, she stopped work and called out, "Where are you going, traveller?"

"I am looking for a land where neither Age nor Death is," he answered.

"Then stay here with me," she said. "It is so long since I talked with anyone."

"Can Age and Death come here?" he asked.

"Not until I have emptied this lake with my sieve."

"Then they will come here, some day," said the Prince, and he rode on.

Many days after that he came to the edge of a vast forest, that spread its varied greens over mountains, and filled valleys as far as he could see in every direction. A woman was striving to cut down a huge tree. She could not have joined her arms round its trunk, but she was trying to cut it down with a pair of little nail scissors. "Where are you going?" she called out to him. "Come and tell me."

"I am looking for a land where neither Age nor Death is," he said.

"Then stay with me. I am so tired and it has been so long since I had company."

"Can Age or Death come here?" he asked.

"They can, but not until I have cut down every tree of this forest with my little scissors."

"Then they will come, one day," said the Prince, and he rode on.

After many days' travel, he came upon a most beautiful sight, and stopped to admire it — a mountain, miles high and miles wide, made all of hard, hard diamond, that flashed and glared brightly in the sun. Shading his eyes, he saw the tiny figure of a woman kneeling beside the mountain. She was scraping away at the mountain's side with a nail-file. "Where are you going?" she asked the Prince.

"I am looking for a land where neither Age nor Death is," he said.

"Then stay here with me – Age and Death will come, but not until I have ground this diamond mountain to dust with my nail-file."

"Then they will come, one day," said the Prince, and rode on.

At last he reached the very ends of the earth, where the winds live. The winds called out to him, "Why have you come here, Prince? There is nothing living here, and nothing for the living."

"I am looking for the land where neither Age nor Death is."

"Then you have found it," said the winds. "It is here."

The Prince could not believe that he had found the land he had been searching for so long. "Is it true that neither Age nor Death comes here?" he cried.

"It is true," said the winds. "Whenever they approach, we blow them away."

"Then here I shall stay," said the Prince. "Here I am safe."

The winds blow over all the earth, and they bring back to their home hundreds and thousands of things that they have collected on their travels, from all times and all places. In a great heap they toss all the forgotten and discarded things: strands of hair, and feathers, pages from books in all languages, shells – bones – barrels and stones and tallies – coins, bits of cloth, dried and dead flowers, lockets, sticks of worn wood. The Prince amused himself by picking through this heap of things finding tools, birds' nests, scent-bottles, rusty nails, broken cups: more things, both rich and odd, drab and ordinary, than any book could list in all its pages. By chance one day he came upon a broken ring, and he recognized it as the seal-ring his father, the King, had worn on his thumb. He cleaned and polished it, and the brighter the ring became, the more he longed to see his father and his home again. "For though I shall live for ever here," he thought to himself, "my father, and everyone I used to know, will die. I will go back and see them all once again." And he called out to the winds, "I am going home. I shall stay there a year or two, and then return."

"You have no home," the winds said. "It has fallen down long ago; it is buried in the earth."

"But I have been here only a few months," said the Prince.

"Your father and your friends are dead," said the winds. "Their children's children are dead. You have been here too long."

"You are telling me lies," said the Prince angrily. "I have not been here a year."

"Neither Age nor Death comes here," said the winds, "but they travel over the earth as they please."

But the Prince would not believe them, and he left the end of the earth and travelled back to his own land. On the way he came to the place where the diamond mountain had been. Only a little stump of it remained, and the woman was still working on it with her nail-file. She saw him and called out, "It has been a long time since I saw you last!"

"I thought it only a year," said the Prince, "but it must have been longer." As he spoke, the woman ground the last bit of the mountain into dust, and the winds came and blew it away. Immediately the woman aged, and died.

The Prince rode on, and came to the place where the forest had been. One tree was still standing. The woman with the nail-scissors saw him and called out, "Prince! It has been a long time since you passed this way."

"I thought it no more than a few years, but it must have been longer," said the Prince and, as he spoke, the woman cut through the last bit of the tree's trunk, and it fell. Immediately the woman aged, and died.

The Prince rode on, and came to the place where the lake had been. There was only a dry bed, and the woman with the sieve was scattering the last drops of water. As she saw him, the last drop fell, and she aged and died.

The Prince rode on, with little hope now, but still looking for his father's palace. Occasionally he would recognize a hill or a river, but the country was changed; the roads sunk deeper, the towns larger, the forests smaller. He reached his home and found only a green hillock where his father's city had been, with no sign of the walls and towers that had once stood there. He dismounted and climbed to the top of the mound, where he found two people sitting in a hollow. They were playing chess, and both stooped over the board so he could not see their faces. One was an old woman with long grey hair. A string of worn-out shoes tied together hung over her shoulder and trailed on the ground behind her. Her companion was a large and bony man, dressed in the long black robes of a monk, with the black hood drawn over his head. On the ground at his side lay a scythe.

Both players were so intent on their game that the Prince stood beside them for a little while, wondering who they were and why they should play chess there, on that hill top. It was not until he shifted a little, and his shadow fell across the playing-board that they noticed him. Both turned their faces towards him.

The woman's face was more wrinkled, creased and raddled than any the Prince had ever seen. The man's face, in the dimness of his hood, seemed to be skin stretched horribly tight over bone.

"Child, at last you have come home!" exclaimed the ancient woman. "Do you know how many years I have spent searching for you, and how many miles I have walked in that search? See how many shoes I have worn out!" She shook the long string of tattered shoes that hung over her shoulder, and reached out suddenly for the Prince's hand, which she gripped as if she would make his hand a part of her own.

The bony man in monk's robes took the Prince's other hand, in a grip equally hard, and as cold as it was strong. "Come with me, and I will take you where your father and brother are," he said.

Then all the years of the Prince's exile aged him, and he died.

Company on the Road

There was once a man named Jack Gabriel who spent every night of his life in the pub, never leaving until it closed, and sometimes not then. Every night he walked home in the dark and barged his way into the house, falling over the furniture and waking his entire family up. His wife had asked him to come home earlier until she was tired of asking, but he paid her no attention. She had asked him to come into the house more quietly, but of that he was incapable when he was drunk.

One winter's night he started home from the pub. The moon shone brightly on the road, and on the ice covering the puddles, but it was not a comforting light. It was shifting and tricky. There was something eerie about that night, and Jack's little dog, which followed him everywhere, began to whimper and bristle. Seeing this, Jack started to whistle and look frequently behind him. He peered closely at tree-stumps standing in the hedge, and at the shadows under trees, and he wished fervently for company on the road.

He turned a bend and saw, ahead of him, the figure of a woman wearing a poke-bonnet and a shawl, and carrying a basket on her arm. "Company for us," he said to his dog. "A nice young woman, by the looks of her. Poor girl. I wonder why she's out so late alone? She'll be glad of the company too, I expect." And he stepped out to catch the young woman, without noticing that his little dog hung back, bristling all the more, and then scrabbled through the hedge and ran away altogether.

Jack caught up with the young woman, and said, "A cold night."

"Yes, a cold night," said the woman, in a beautiful, deep, soft young woman's voice. Jack was delighted. He couldn't see her face, because the poke of her bonnet hid it from him, but he was sure that, if her voice was so beautiful, her face must be too.

"A nasty night for you to be out all on your own, m' dear," he said.

"Oh, I had to come out. My grandmother is sick, and needs me."

"Haven't you got no husband, nor brothers, nor a father to walk with you, then, m' dear?" Jack asked.

"Oh no," she sighed. "I'm all alone in the world."

"Well, my dear, I'm that sorry," Jack said. "Here – let me carry the basket for you."

He took the basket from her, and her soft, deep voice said, "Thank you very much; you are so kind" – but he felt the basket quiver with the sound. The voice came from inside the *basket*, not the bonnet.

Jack was cold from the winter's night; now he went cold to the centre of his bones. He turned his head and looked at the young woman walking beside him, so pretty and nice. As if she knew he was looking at her, she turned her head too and, for the first time, Jack saw past the wide brim of her poke-bonnet – and the bonnet was quite empty.

"The Headless Boggart!" Jack cried aloud, and in a tremble of horror, he dropped the basket. The white cloth covering it fell away and from inside there rolled out, on to the frosty road, a woman's pretty head, laughing in a deep, soft woman's voice.

Jack started running. He pounded along the road to his home, his heart swinging and thudding inside him – and behind him he heard the swift tapping of the Headless Boggart's running feet. Then worse – he heard a woman's laughter, and past him came rolling the woman's head. He saw the whites of its eyes shine as it rolled them round to see him. The head rolled under his feet, trying to trip him, and desperately he leaped in the air, to avoid it. The head leaped too, and snapped its teeth at his heels.

But Jack jumped clear and ran on. He crashed at

full tilt into the door of his house, yelling for his wife to let him in – which she did, and his little shivering dog too.

Jack had to spend three days in bed recovering from that night, and for all his life after he was careful never to be out so late again.

All Jack's wife would say about it was that the Boggart must be a very clever little madam indeed, since it had taught Jack to come home early and half-sober. That was more than she, his wife, had ever been able to do, for all she carried a good head on her shoulders instead of in a basket.

GHOSTS THAT HAUNT YOU
ed. Aidan Chambers

Bumps, squeaks and terror in the moonlight. Sometimes funny, sometimes horrifying, this superb collection of spooky stories all involve children in some way.

A CHRISTMAS CARD
Paul Theroux

A wonderfully eerie story! Driving down from the city, parents and two young boys go hopelessly astray in the snow and dark, but at last they find welcoming shelter for the night in a strange old mansion. 'This place is so far from anywhere that you have to be lost before you find it,' said their host, a tall man in a cloak. He is nowhere to be seen when they leave in the morning but he has left them a card – and it is the boy Marcel who first perceives that this card is a kind of map, what's more a *living* map.

THE DRIFTWAY
Penelope Lively

The Driftway is a strange road, a travelling road, centuries old. For those who choose to hear them, there are messages along the Driftway – echoes from the past. On the run from home with his little sister, Paul thumbs a lift on old Bill's horse-drawn cart, but as they slowly travel down the Driftway the messages come and Paul begins to see something special for him in each one. A fascinating and strangely haunting novel.

KEPT IN THE DARK
Nina Bawden

Clara and Bosie and Noel all found the big strange isolated house and the grandparents they'd never met before rather daunting. And when David turned up and claimed he belonged there too, things got even more disturbing. There were so many secrets to find the answers to.

THE CLOCK TOWER GHOST
Gene Kemp

Addlesbury Tower is haunted by Rich King Cole, a mean old man who fell off it long ago in mysterious circumstances. Its newest terror is Mandy – feared by her family and eventually by the ghost too. In the war they wage to dominate the tower, Mandy and King Cole do frightful and funny things to each other, little guessing how much they really have in common.

THE GHOST OF THOMAS KEMPE
Penelope Lively

Strange messages, fearful noises and all kinds of jiggery-pokery! It began to dawn on James that there was probably a ghost in the house. But what kind of ghost was it that had come to plague the Harrison family in their lovely old cottage? James sets out to find the answer in this delightfully funny story.

GHOSTS, SPOOKS AND SPECTRES
ed. Charles Molin

From the pens of Charles Dickens, H. G. Wells, James Thurber, Sir Arthur Conan Doyle and many other master storytellers, come these phantoms of the night, bringing secrets from beyond the grave. Eighteen tales – some disturbing, some amusing and some downright terrifying!

THE GHOST DOWNSTAIRS
Leon Garfield

Mr Fast signs away the last seven years of his life in return for the riches of the world – but gets more than he bargained for!

THE GHOST'S COMPANION
ed. Peter Haining

Thrilling ghost stories by well-known writers – and the incidents which first gave them the idea.

GHOSTLY GALLERY
ed. Alfred Hitchcock

A bumper collection of ghost stories – some are not too serious, some are even funny, but most of them are chilling and spooky. But what else would you expect from Alfred Hitchcock?

MESSAGES
Marjorie Darke

How would *you* feel if you came face to face with a ghostly character on a Fun Run – or a flying broomstick with a mind of its own, a pony that keeps vanishing or a skeleton that is certainly not prepared to stay in a cupboard? – This is a spooky collection which will send shivers down your spine for sure!

TAKE THE LONG PATH
Joan de Hamel

The story of David, a New Zealand boy, and his strange friendship with an old Maori man.

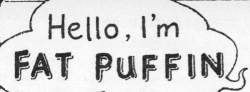

Hello, I'm FAT PUFFIN

Would YOU like to find out more about Puffin books and authors, enter competitions and get a chance to buy new books?

Then join The Puffin Club!

You will get a copy of the Club magazine four times a year, a membership book and a badge.

And there's lots more! For further details and an application form send a stamped, addressed envelope to:

The Puffin Club,
P.O. Box 21,
Cranleigh,
Surrey,
GU6 8UZ

If you live in AUSTRALIA write to: The Australian Puffin Club, Penguin Books Australia Ltd., P.O. Box 257, Ringwood, Victoria 3134